Dragons, Cowboys, and Other Mythical Creatures

by Linda Crichton

The contents of this work, including, but not limited to, the accuracy of events, people, and places depicted; opinions expressed; permission to use previously published materials included; and any advice given or actions advocated are solely the responsibility of the author, who assumes all liability for said work and indemnifies the publisher against any claims stemming from publication of the work.

All Rights Reserved
Copyright © 2019 by Linda Crichton

No part of this book may be reproduced or transmitted, downloaded, distributed, reverse engineered, or stored in or introduced into any information storage and retrieval system, in any form or by any means, including photocopying and recording, whether electronic or mechanical, now known or hereinafter invented without permission in writing from the publisher.

Dorrance Publishing Co
585 Alpha Drive
Pittsburgh, PA 15238
Visit our website at *www.dorrancebookstore.com*

ISBN: 978-1-4349-1515-3
eISBN: 978-1-4349-1430-3

A Carpenter

A Carpenter He was
God's only begotten son
Perfect in all He does
Teaching to everyone

Healing the sick
Miracles He did
Disciples He did pick
Nothing He hid

More than a man
Savior to the world
The only one that can
In prison He was hurled

On the cross He died
Three days He rose to be
Savior! He's on our side
Jesus Christ is He!

Fallen Race

2030 was the year
Finally, the war was over
So many shed a tear
People still watched for a Rover

Lightning flashes across the sky
Rain falls on a lone scarecrow
Here fallen soldiers still lie
Blood on a plow, where wheat did grow

Brave men with courage so bold
Brought freedom to this fallen race
They broke the Emperor's evil hold
Soldiers fighting bravely face   to face

Devastation of the land is vast
But the storm gives people some hope
They can rebuild their fallen past
Pulling together the people can cope

Fall Of Darkness

Darkness has fallen
Hiding the best I can
Someone was callin'
It was not a sane man

I turned to fight
Shaking hands and sweaty palms
Keeping my rifle in tight
I threw some bombs

Creeping and then running
Then finally stopping
Using all of my cunning
Hearing far off popping

Finding the old caves
Soon I would be out of this mess
My message sent on air waves
My mission was a success

Even Angels Get Tired

One little angel wouldn't go to sleep
All she wanted to do was play
Out of bed she would always creep
She was getting so tired each new day

The other angels tried everything
But nothing seemed to help
They didn't know what to bring
We have tried everything, they cried with a yelp

The angels went and got advice
We have done all we know to do
They even gave the little angel white mice
One angel got an idea so away she flew

Later the angel returned from her trip
She brought a very big gift with care
To the gift the little angel, did zip
Little angel asleep, finally on a huge Teddy Bear

Escape

Creeping out his door
Into the moonlit night
Leaving home forever more
He turned on his flashlight

Everyone had already gone
He had to cover their tracks
He had miles to go before dawn
He checked all his packs

Danger would be here soon
He set several of his traps
Carefully heading for a dune
There he checked his maps

He heard a crash and a cry
He melted into the shadowy brush
He silently crept on by and by
Hearing nothing but a quiet hush

Earthly Sonnet

Rains brings a beautiful rainbow
Dark clouds cover majestic mountains
Rivers race on where they flow
Sending water to city fountains

Sun brings rays of delight
To warm an island land
Birds take to flight
As an animal walks the sand

Trees in a dark forest stand
Turning into a meadow green
Eating quietly there a deer band
Watching for danger still unseen

Desert with its mysterious ways
Coyotes howl in the night
Where man hardly stays
Everything is in God's sight

An Empty Pocket

I remember my grandma telling
Of a little orphan boy with an empty pocket
It was hard times, lots of folks yelling
The boy's only treasure was his mother's locket

My grandma knew him a long time ago
Our neighbor took some kids in
A pox epidemic hit to and fro
It killed a lot of women and men

Then people found a cure
And several lives were saved
It helped all to endure
It brought people closer in what they braved

People helped each other
It really wasn't a bother
Things got better for one another
The orphan boy was my grandfather

Celebrate

The age of freedom is born
The song of America is sung
We celebrate and toot our own horn
There are bells also to be rung

Parades start off the grand day
Family picnics by the lake
Everyone is excited and gay
Games to play and ribbons to take

The fun never ends at the fair
For the 4th of July is here
Riding the carnival rides, if you dare
Every event is now in full gear

Finally! Fireworks brilliantly light the sky!
People watch with ohs and ahs
Our flag of red, white and blue waves high
Freedom we take a silent moment to pause

Days Gone By

The rustling of the leaves
The smell of pine trees
Rain dripping off the eaves
The buzzing of the honey bees

Scent of lilac in the air
Tiger lilies giving a little sway
Biting a sour apple, if you dare
The tractor busily cutting hay

Chickens and turkeys in their pen
The cat showing off her kittens
Grandpa filling the old coal bin
Grandma on the porch knitting mittens

Jumping off my old blue bike
Running up the stairs so fast
Telling them what things I like
These are memories of a childhood past

Yo Ho Ho

Gentle sea breeze
Dawn does break
Moving by degrees
Slowly I wake

Beautiful island scene
Swaying palm tree
Everything so green
I'm so free

Sailing the sea
Treasure to find
For only me
Luck is kind

Treasure I've won
Fight not flee
Timmy dinners on
Mom is calling me

Two Friends

Mom, what can I do?
I like him so much
But! He says we're through
I miss talking to Dutch

He's been a good friend
We like the same things
I don't know if I'll mend
We wear each other's rings

Mom was saying, as she hugged me
Friends are going to fight
It will be alright, you'll see
Why don't you talk, make it alright

Dutch was knocking at the door
"Sorry Abby! Want to ride bikes?"
Abby said, "I'm glad you're not mad anymore"
We rode to get ice cream at Mike's

True Hero

In shadows one man stands
For he is a hero true
He was there with helping hands
Doing what he had to do

The other man took the praise
He didn't even lift a finger
Walking around in a hero's daze
Fame he liked it to linger

In the shadows one man waits
Knowing the truth of the matter
Thinking of the twist of fates
He was not like the latter

As good faces down evil men
In the shadow heroes are true
Evil thinking of how to win
Good with courage and braver just do

Helping Hand

One summer I went to Grandma's house
I was thirteen and I didn't need a babysitter
Nothing to do but watch Tabby catch a mouse
Help Grandma pick up all the yard litter

Grandma was there to meet me at the train
We hugged and kissed and talked awhile
She handed me a locket on a chain
Thank you! I gave my best smile

A storm was a brewin' so we hurried in
I laughed, Grandma still had her assorted pets
We checked all the animals in every pen
Can we name the new colt Storm? Let's

Grandma twisted her ankle back to the house
We put her foot up on a cushiony stand
Earlier I had complained, I felt like a louse
Grandma said, I was her helping hand

Time

Time has a way of changing things
Life changes us too with time
You never know what life brings
Time passes with each little chime

Kids are in a hurry to grow up
The older ones wish they were young
Stories to be told, when I was a pup
With songs to be sung

Time can be a fleeting moment
Or one hour seems to last forever
Time can be spent with enjoyment
All of us work tell the time of never

Good times or bad, we live them all
Our memories are our past
Our future is God's call
Life is for living, it goes by fast

The Waiting Danger

The rain forest was quiet and dark
A black panther waited in a tree
He was waiting for an easy mark
Look as he might nothing could he see

The panther decided to hunt else where
Animals came out from where they were hidden
But, always watching with great care
The danger they would not be ridden

The rain forest home was a nice place
But, you had to have a good nose
A cobra used a tree as his base
He liked to lay up there and doze

Some animals hid in the ruins of stone
Or some made homes in the cave wall
There enemies never leave them along
Each has its own special signal call

The Surprise

Walking down the dirt road
I was down to my last dime
Everything was dry, like an old toad
I was just not having a good time

I saw some workers in a field
So I went to see about a job
We worked until the dinner bell pealed
We had a great meal, even corn on the cob

I worked all summer there
I was back on the road again
Walking on without a care
Going home to see my kin

No one really expected me
I did odd jobs along the way
I bought some gifts for a small fee
I made it home on Christmas Day!

The Stranger

One stormy night
Walking down the road
He was surrounded by light
He carried a light load

No one seemed to see him
No one seemed to care
The world looked dim
People that saw would only stare

Joe stopped, giving him a ride
Ask him in for the night
He had nothing to hide
He was gone with the morning light

He had come to find the good
He found but only a very few
Finding those few our world still stood
If he comes, what will you do?

Snow Country

Pine trees sway
As a blizzard rages
Snow piles up all day
Like it's done through the ages

The storm moves on
The sun shines through
The snow will soon be gone
Sparkling snow looked brand new

Last great storm of the season
Spring is a time of blooming
It happens without rhyme or reason
Flowers would soon be looming

A rabbit looking for a grass stubble
While a coyote silently watches him
Going in his hole, sensing some trouble
Coyote's supper looked quite dim

Silver Writer

With silver pen in hand
He writes his story down
Writing dreams about the land
Stories about his own town

The silver ink is flowing
His thoughts put on paper
He keeps the story going
Plot thickens in a mysterious caper

Secret is his own name
Silver writer writes on
Stories are never the same
The suspense is never gone

Silver ink writes the hero
Several villains are in there
He may even write of Nero
Read his stories if you dare

Seal's Tale

Whispering in the dark
Thinking we may be lost
Sounds of a lonely lark
We must fight at any cost

Down on one knee
Hoping God will hear
No enemy do we see
Forward with great fear

Waiting for the dawn
We inch our way along
We are only a pawn
Crickets sing their song

Guns come suddenly alive
We hear wounded cry
Battle won so we strive
Silence surrounds where we lie

Rebels with a Cause

Our planes flew in formation
Over dark ocean waters
Flying for our great nation
For America's sons and daughters

Rebels with a great cause
To free a people enslaved
There is no room for pause
The innocent to be saved

Bombs are at the ready
Soon our target is in view
We fly on our hands steady
Bombs dropped, away we flew

Planes going back to base
Our strike is a success
Cheers and smiles on every face
Freedom we'll take nothing less

Momma's Story

Momma? Would you tell us a story?
What story do you want to hear?
One about angels, said Lori
Cory said, Are angels and Heaven very near?

They fly anywhere on feathered wing
Beings beautifully dressed in white
Angels also love to sing
They are surrounded by golden light

Angels live in Heaven with God
Heaven is quite far from here
But, to our story, she said with a nod
Two children playing followed a deer

They were lost deep in the wood
An angel came taking them by the hand
Soon at home they stood
Smiling, looking in the window, a small angel band

Heart of Hearts

Hearts soar like a dove
My heart can confide
For only one love
To be your bride

Together we are one
Dancing close in time
Tell the music is done
Making our own rhyme

A promise from both
With a golden band
Each with loves oath
Taking me by the hand

My heart of hearts
Sealed with a kiss
Our lives soon starts
For a Heavenly bliss

Loves Word

How can I tell you
How much I care
With so many words
How do I dare

Words can never express
The love I have for you
Words are just spoken
But it's all in what you do

With One little word
My heart can be broken
A touch of your hand
Not a word was spoken

Looking deep in your eyes
Love is looking back at me
With a sudden embrace
I've given my hearts key

Living Life

Life has been hard
Bitter with the sweet
Just a little bit scarred
Still on our feet

We fight to live
Work tell we bleed
Still we will give
In word and deed

Weary in our heart
Standing for the right
Doing our own part
Still we will fight

Taking time to breathe
Wiping sweat with a sweep
That's life we weave
Memories we do keep

Irish Goodbye

Gone for the day
I wish you were here
I know you couldn't stay
I'll wipe away a tear

I love you still
You will never return
I know it is God's will
Still I will always yearn

I know it is for the best
The pain is over now
Pipes play at your rest
I'll remember you is my vow

You'll be gone for a little while
Please, do remember me
I'll miss your beautiful smile
My love you will always be

Home On the Range

Home on the range
As the old saying goes
Being in a city, that seems strange
Maybe an island, who knows

A desert land, it's too hot
Down under, might fit
A swamp, definitely not
You might get bit

High on a mountain top
That would be the place
It couldn't be a bus stop
Or on a smooth cliff face

Home on the range
It's not a quiz
You don't need to change
Home is where the heart is

Hip, Hip, Hooray

Hooray! For America we say
And for those that were freed
That was a great, great day
The soldiers deserve honor for that deed

Soldiers who died we are so proud
Some soldiers can now come home
We honor these with pride and heads bowed
Each getting shining medals of chrome

So stand up and cheer, my friend
For we are also still free
And we will be true to the end
For honor and glory America shall be

God has blessed us in this way
Hooray! For America for which she stands
Our beloved America is here to stay
We wave our flag in these great lands

Growing Up

In the pines a little house stood
By a lovely babbling brook
On the porch was piled some fire wood
It was a pretty cozy little nook

A big red barn was nearby
With corrals all around it
Here is where the milk cows lie
Sleeping tell the sun gets up a bit

The rooster crows his morning song
Breakfast is set on the table
Work to do all day long
Soon its getting horses from the stable

Dad is out catching our old mule
Children's chores are all done
So soon they are off to school
Waving goodbye to everyone

Grandpa

Grandpa worked on the railroad
Helping to lay down the tracks
Building bridges where rivers flowed
Carrying supplies in with packs

It was hard but honest work
Falling in bed at night
Waking to smell the coffee perk
Breakfast was before the morning light

Blasting through mountain sides
Working in all kinds of weather
Wearing clothes of animal hides
They all work hard together

Rarely getting home to see their wives
Tracks were laid with their sweat
Good men lost their lives
Years later tracks soon met

Gone Fishin'

Every summer my dad and I went fishin'
But one summer Dad was too busy
So I picked a star and started wishin'
Mom and Dad were always in a tizzy

I decided something else must be wrong
The hardware store, one day I went
A job I wanted, I walked right along
I can work How old are you Mr. Trent?

I'm eight, my mom and dad need money
Well, I'll go talk to your father
Mr. Green closed the store, let's go sonny
He and Dad talked, finally saying, No bother

Mr. Green made Dad a partner at his store
I got a hug, I'd accomplished my mission
We both went to work, I sweep the floor
Today the hardware store sign reads, GONE FISHIN'

Going No Where

I'm on a train for nowhere
I just want to get away
Where I don't really care
It's been a bad day

My heart feels broken
So here I am
My tears are unspoken
Why did I still love, Sam?

Our words were pretty bitter
The end is never sweet
I've never been a quitter
I feel like I'm pretty beat

Is this seat taken, miss?
There he was on one knee!
He gave me a kiss
Please! Forgive me, will you marry me?

God Waits

As God sits in Heaven above
He sees the fight between evil and good
Hoping each person will feel his love
Waiting for his words to be understood

God arms us with ammunition for the fight
If we will just listen and learn
He guides us with Heavenly sight
Seeking his wisdom as a child, we yearn

God's word is simple, without fuss
Jesus Christ, is our Savior and our brother
God never gives up on each of us
We shouldn't give up on each other

Our eyes are the windows to our souls
We all are seeking inner peace
Each person has different ideas and goals
May our hopes and dreams never cease

Friends

Friends are kind and loving souls
Some can be with you life-long
They take on sister or brother roles
Fighting over things, when things go wrong

Friends know us so well
You're always there for each other
Keeping secrets, they won't tell
Fighting off bullies like a big brother

Friends cry with us at that certain time
Giving a kind and warm helping hand
Success together, we make the difficult climb
Helping a friend in return is so grand

Friends are God's special gift from the heart
Keeping a friendship both of us strives
Goodbyes, are hard when friends drift apart
Friends are a wonderful part of our lives

Freedom's Right

Flag flying
Hand salute
Men trying
Army boot

Guns sound
Unwritten pages
Enemy found
War rages

Fierce battle
Men fall
Bombs rattle
Fighting all

Brave men
Moonlit night
Triumphant win
Freedoms Right

Freedom

Once a long time ago
Our forefathers sailed to a new land
Banished by an English foe
Who ruled them with an iron hand

But peace was not meant to be
To arms rang out for freedoms plight
As the king's battleships were put to sea
Soon brave men gathered to stand and fight

We won our freedom that is true
As a new flag flew over head
Colors of red, white and blue
And English soldiers turned and fled

The Constitution was wrote in cabin hall
So we could still be free in this great land
We shout liberty and justice for all
One nation under God we stand

A Father's Love

Dad called us one sunny day
All three of us ran into the room
You're old enough to work not play
He handed all of us a broom

First two older brothers said no
We're going away to get richer pay
Hurt in my father's eyes, he said go
Dad, I'm still here to stay

Thanks son! You now own everything
Wow! I stayed and helped my Dad
Clearing fields to work, rocks to sling
Learning about life and work from a lad

Sometime later my brothers came home
They both looked ragged but a lot smarter
Dad welcomed them, never did they roam
I handed them a broom for a starter

A Cold and Eerie Tale

Come and I'll tell you a tale
Of a horrible ghostly being
It will almost make your heart fail
It's not for everyday sight seeing

One foggy and cold winter's night
Outlaws made themselves a camp
Hiding from the laws sight
Building no fire although they were damp

The outlaws killed just for the fun of it
Evil was their only way
They passed the bottle around getting lit
They were the Devil's own you might say

Suddenly! Out of the fog came a horse
A old man rode him dressed in white
Something hit the outlaws with great force
Each outlaw was on fire growing bright

Screaming! The outlaws rolled on the ground
Surprised! Agony was on their tortured faces
The strange fire kept burning them all around
Sentenced are you! Your bones leave no traces

Sheriff finding the camp hearing a screaming sound
Seeing the old man with glowing red eyes
The old man said, They are sentenced and bound
He then disappeared to the sheriff's surprise

A Fast One

Mail must get through
Cowboys rough around the edges
Riding hard and fast was nothing new
Riding even along narrow ledges

Riding horses half wild
Hoping to have a fast one
And not to get a pony riled
They ride until the job is done

Indians did attack
Some were killed
Some had the knack
Getting through if God willed

It took several days
They rode tried and true
They deserve our praise
Pony Express did get through

The Harsh Land

Black clouds filled the sky
As a cowboy spotted a place to camp
He heard the winds moaning cry
He reckoned it would get pretty damp

The desert could be a harsh land
If a man wasn't careful here he would die
It was full of cactus and sand
Where only a few old buzzards fly

Today a storm had been brewin'
Great sheets of rain came down
The cowboy was dry in a old Indian ruin
This was once a busy Indian town

The cowboy knew the signs well
Flash flood was on its way
As sheets of rain still fell
The cowboy was safe and sound where he lay

Black Monster

Cowboys riding hard that night
Caught in the rain and the wind
Lightning makes everything light
Hoping to make the next bend

The tornado is tearing up the ground
The wind is like a howling beast
It's a horrible deafening sound
Black Monster eating a great feast

Horses screaming, on cowboys ride
Reaching a deep gully, they fled
Riding into the gully to hide
As the tornado howls over head

The tornado moves on its deadly trail
Horses and cowboys have survived
They can still hear the awful wail
Later they ride home, glad to be alive

Cowboy and the Rose

Riding hard across the desert land
How long could he stay ahead of them
For after him was a fierce Apache band
For the cowboy things looked grim

Suddenly! His horse stumbled and fell
They were both tumbling down a sandy hill
Apaches watched, finally riding on with a yell
Horse and cowboy survived the steep spill

Dazed, he made sure the Indians were gone
The only thing broken is the water canteen
The cowboy rode several days until one dawn
His mind played tricks on what he'd seen

Laughing, he grabbed at a beautiful pink rose
The rose turned into a woman pointing away
Stumbling that way finally, falling on his nose
His hand fell in water, where he lay

Cowboy Flight

As I took my daily walk
I saw a very old passenger train
It was a tour train so was the talk
I decided to buy a ticket, thinking myself insane

I picked up a brochure as I waited
It read, Ride! To an Old Wild West Town!
The train was 1880, so it was dated
I got on the train and sat down

Here I go to spend an enjoyable day
We arrived just a little late
Everyone was now in western dress and went their way
Odd! It looked so real it took me back to the 1880 date

Strange, I was alone no tour guide in sight
So, I went in search of some real western food
Passing a saloon, where two men were in a fight
Eatery up ahead! It put me in a lighter mood

The man brought meat, beans and beer
The jail was next with all its fame
The sheriff talked to me about hunting deer
The sheriff and my name were the same

People started yelling, as shots were fired!
You'll have to do as a deputy, don't get shot!
By the time it was over, we were both tired
If you want a job, you're hired and thanks a lot

Thanks! But I have a train to be on
We shook hands and I headed for the train
Dazed! I looked back and it was all gone!
A star, home and the sheriff, my grandfather waiting in the lane

Cowboy in Heaven

With hat in hand
I stood before the Lord
Angels around me in a small band
One with a fiery sword

It was a glorious place
I realized I must be dead
I'm actually seeing God face to face!
A scroll was being read

The scroll was about me
God asked me to come and sit
A book was put on my knee
Read this, it will take you a bit

I have a job for you to do
I need you to get in my cattle
We have cowboys you knew
Heaven isn't bad as I sat my saddle

Cowboy Life

I ride an old paint
I'm true to the brand
This cowboy ain't no saint
But I'm a pretty fair hand

A cowboy is my life
For very little pay
I can use a gun or knife
Honest is my way

Workin' hard all day
Fences to always mend
Cuttin' and puttin' up hay
Cows to gather around the bend

Some nights I sleep under the stars
Using my saddle for my pillow
Eating breakfast from mason jars
Watching the sunrise in the willow

Cowboy Prayer

If I die and get to go to Heaven
I'd like to have my spurs and boots
Ride my old black horse, Seven
I don't want one of those fancy suits

I hope they have cows up there
So this cowboy can keep on workin'
Rope and ride without a care
Keep those old cows a perkin'

I tried to live by the right
I've had a good life
I love God with all my might
Never had time for a wife

I'm an ornery old cuss
Broke a bone a time or two
I don't want a big fuss
Lord, I'll work hard for you

Echoes

As the sunset
On a small town
Rain made the street wet
It really came down

Silent was the street
No one lives here
A mouse enjoyed a treat
Without any kind of fear

Gold rush long gone
In a harsh land
Passing into a new dawn
Fate played out its hand

Echoes of those forgotten times
Whisper of ghostly voices
Church bell gently chimes
Midnight brings strange noises

Indian Wisdom

I'm a cowboy who likes to hunt and guide
And a friend to the local Indian camp
The chief gave me a necklace with pride
I wear it wherever I roam or tramp

One winter I guided for a Russian Prince
He was a good shot, sure surprised me
We got to be good friends, me and Vince
Elk, deer and buffalo, we would see

Vince shot an elk, when! Avalanche! Everyone run!
Running, I sure wish we were back at camp!
Zap! We were back at camp, everyone!
Turning round, my foot I did stamp

Several days later, I talked to the chief
Grinning, he said, the necklace was protecting me
The Great Spirit gives power, if only brief
That power saved me several times, you see

Pecos and Cactus

Pecos Bill is a tough cowboy
Legend tells he can do anything
Riding his horse, Widowmaker, is his great joy
They can almost fly on eagles wing

Cactus Pete is a bad outlaw
He fights Pecos Bill all the time
Cactus Pete is a gunfighter, fast on the draw
He lives his life only for crime

Cactus Pete robs the train
Or he likes robbing the bank
Cactus Pete is definitely insane
His life is pretty dank

Pecos Bill can do no wrong
He puts Cactus Pete in jail
That's where bad men belong
Pecos Bill will never fail

Old Red

The cowboy put on his baggy pants
He painted his face white, red and black
He rehearsed his funny little dance
Taking his wig and hat off the rack

Well, reckon I'm ready, he said
So off he went with the other clown
They were introduced as Pete and Red
Keeping wild bulls off cowboys while they were down
A cowboy could get hurt or killed
Red had been hurt a time or two
Cowboys were kept safe as the crowds were thrilled
Making people laugh, they like to do

As a clown this was Reds last year
So after the rodeo Red got an award
Thanks a lot! Waving, Red wiped away a tear
Red did his dance as the crowd roared

Scared

The wind has an eerie sound
Blowing across the barren plain
Across dark snow covered ground
Sounding like a animal in pain

Cowboys listen to the wind
Shadowy figures dance by the firelight
Horses they have to tend
Keeping the herd of cows in sight

Cowboys' skin began to prickle
As ghost drums began to beat
Scared! One rubbed his lucky nickel
Guns gathered, to see what they'd meet

Sounds of Indians came in the air
Morning came none to soon
Cowboys were glad they had their hair
They were long gone before noon

Shadows

One dark and stormy night
An eerie wind did blow
Suddenly! A burst of light
It came from a firelight glow

Shimmering shadows play and dance
A hand stirred a boiling pot
Nothing else did you see at a glance
A voice said, This is all I got

The cowboy had fed his horse
He rolled out his bed
As the storm took its course
He ate his beans and hard bread

Soon came the morning light
He packed his gear with great care
Suddenly! A burst of light so bright
Cowboy and horse disappeared in thin air

Silent

The west is wild and untamed
Where ghosts are said to walk
For its outlaws it is famed
So is the stories and the talk

Cowboys spirits roams the land
Forgotten by or disappeared in the past
Blown here or there by the sand
Never seemingly to rest, there cast

Good and the bad are among the few
Searching for something they can't find
Doing things the way they used to do
Replaying events in their own mind

The wind blows their forgotten names
As they ride their mustangs across the sky
This land they ride to make their claims
Forever the ghostly figures fly

The Savage Tale

He's silently walking
On fallen snow
Killer is stalking
Knowing his foe

Silent ever silently
Slowly he goes
Heart beating violently
He's about froze

Down a hill
Into a wood
Everything is still
There it stood

Taking a breath
Arrow is shot
Causing its death
Buffalo he got

The Warrior

Wild and free am I
I go wherever I want
To climb the mountain high
Elk and deer to hunt

My ceiling is the clouds and sky
Meadows and hills are my home
The mossy grass is where I lie
The trees are where I can roam

I can sit where eagles fly
I have felt the storms fury
Here I live and will die
No need to get in a hurry

So stands a warrior strong and true
For a warriors life is free
Protect the things I love I'll do
This is where I want to be

Thundering Hooves

The thundering hooves across the prairie
Wild horses mustangs, they're called
Here is where they live and tarry
Part of the old west, naturally installed

Indians and cowboys have rode them
Some mustangs couldn't be ridden
They go wherever they take a whim
Most mustangs stay lost or hidden

Mustangs are a part of history
Horses are still ridden today
Mustangs are somewhat of a mystery
Here in the old west they stay

Mustangs come in any color or size
But there's no horse meaner or rougher
And usually never seen by human eyes
Surviving in this land makes them tougher

Trail Seekers

Across the prairie they came
In covered wagons or on horse back
White dots all looking the same
With all their possessions they could pack

Dreams of riches, silver and gold
Some in search of their own lands
So on their wagons rolled
Fighting off Indian bands

Some died along the way
Hopes and dreams were terribly shattered
There on the prairie some still stay
Others kept going bruised and battered

On around the very last bend
To finally see their new home
Their adventures were at an end
But others, yes others, still roam

Willow Butte

Willow Butte is my home
It has been for many a year
I just had to travel and roam
I trapped and panned for gold

Indians I trade with them
So life is pretty good
Every day I'd go to the mountain rim
Looking around there I stood

Seeing sights most people will never see
Spring I travel to the valley below
Trading for coffee, flour and sugar, for me
Back up after a month I go

An Indian wife I married
So my life is pretty complete
Willow Butte now I tarry
My wife makes moccasins for my feet

WindWalker's War Party

Spirits of the world are all around
Windwalkers seeing through eyes of a spirit
Flying through the air or on the ground
Medicine man with great powers, hear it

Good and evil still battle it out
Spirits ride on fiery steeds for the fight
Getting all their weapons for such a bout
Thunder rolls over the sky with flashes of light

Clash of the spirit warriors as they battle
The wind blows the eerie sound
Screams of battle cries as chants rattle
Earthward the spirits are bound

Fireballs are thrown through the air
The ground shakes with great upheaval
Spirit warriors lash out with cold stare
Dawn comes as good is triumphant over evil

Winter's Day

Geese flew over head
Past a frozen lake
On to a watery bed
Noise they did make

Flying in special Vs
Landing in a creek
Icicles hung from trees
Ground hard as a brick

Silent was a fox
Thinking of a goose lunch
He slipped on some rocks
Startled! Flying in a bunch

Fox barked his cry
As the geese flew away
He watched them fly
He'd try again another day

Workin' Rhyme

Cowboy's work is never done
I get up at the break of dawn
Eating my breakfast on the run
Before the sun is up, I'm gone

I catch and saddle my old brown horse
I have some cows to fed and brand
Fences to mend, it's par for the course
My skin gets pretty well tanned

Calves are cute and bulls are tough
A cowboy keeps them in line
Breaking wild horse can be pretty rough
But a cowboy usually breaks them just fine

Summer time is cuttin' and puttin' up hay
Winter you have a little more play time
Workin' hard is just the cowboy way
So ends this cowboy's workin' rhyme

Yellow Stuff

Gold! Was the call
Along the California coast
People wanting a big haul
Gold was not for most

Riches people went crazy for
Wasted lives just to look
Always wanting more and more
Getting rich by being a crook

Racing to find the yellow stuff
Misery ran deep in town
Life could get pretty rough
Some never came back down

Gold fever it was called
Smart ones never went broke
Gold they found and hauled
But all were just plain folk

Memory Book

If I could go back in time
All my family I could see
I could be a kid, that's no crime
But my memories are my only key

My dad was a cowboy
My mom was from the city
My sister took my favorite toy
My grandparents were quite witty

We lived on a small ranch
It was a great place to grow up
We had a few trees to climb on, every branch
We had lots of animals, even a pup

Mom was sweet and like no other
We helped Dad when he had work by the ton
We are still there for one another
I love them all everyone

Memories Past

A lone pine tree stands
On the wild prairie
Forgotten by human hands
Where once people did tarry

Once a little house stood
Bustling and teaming with life
Living the best they could
One full of hard work and strife

Planting a little pine tree
Growing into quite a giant
Now only the tree do you see
Looking so very defiant

A woman got out of a car
Hello! Old tree, she said
Tears in her eyes, she'd come far
Planting another tree where her kin did homestead

Hanks Story

Cowboys were gathering some cows one day
Branding calves, quite a few this year
When two cows and a calf got away
Headed my pony, yellin, I'm goin' over here

Ridin after the cows into a canyon bend
Once I caught a glimpse of them
I found no cows, just a dead end
A big crack in the wall, it looked dim

Riding my pony on through to a green valley
There were the cows knee deep in water
This was like a dream, get along, Sally
This was some place, it's getting hotter

Pushing the cows back through the crack
Ear splitting noise, a giant lizard! It couldn't be!
Another one was by the crack, ready to attack
Lizards fought, I escape, they couldn't follow me

The Dragon and The Wizard

The dragon and the wizard stood talking
By a fallen castle wall
You must listen! Thimakin, stop mocking!
The wizard smiled, We'll go to the hall

But first my castle needs a little repair
Raising his arms, the castle now stood
Zurses just shook his head, without care
Please! Hurry! Thimakin, if you would!

Snapping his fingers, They now stood at the door
See Zurses, We are just in time
The Old One is just coming to the floor
They sat in back to hear the crime

The Old Dragon spoke of the kingdoms fall
The Sea Lord has got to be stopped
Or it will be the ruin of us all
Suddenly! A pink gas was everywhere, everyone dropped

Thimakin and Zurses had seen the pink mist
And were now standing outside
What has happened? Zurses hissed
Gas! said Thimakin, Throwing the doors open wide

Everyone soon stood outside, unharmed
It's a warning only, the Old One said
No need for panic or to be alarmed
It wasn't poisonous, we aren't dead

The Old Dragon told Thimakin of his plan
Thimakin and Zurses said, They would try
Zon and Bellock would help, if they can
Going to get the Topaz Crystal, they did fly

Thimakin and Zurses got to the stone
Zon and Bellock lured out the Sea Lord
Thimakin raised his arms and started to moan
The Sea Lord saw his mistake and roared

The Topaz Crystal spinning wildly now
Was pulling the Sea Lord towards it
The Crystal disappeared, Thimakin wiped his brow
They had heard the screaming when the Sea Lord hit

The Sea Lord and crew were gone
Thimakin weary slumped to the ground
The Sea Lord was back in realm Kron
Dragon and Wizard now homeward bound

The Duel

Sword in hand
Both skilled with a blade
Only one will stand
Both love a lovely maid

The duel was about to begin
The maid was not there
Gathered around were a few men
Each with a cold stare

Both men readied their sword
The cloth was dropped
Just as someone roared
Everyone just suddenly stopped

Look! Isn't that the girl?
She was riding off with another!
She's riding off with the Earl!
Surprised! Both laughed, She was with their
Brother

An Irish Yarn

Two old friends were talking
They were both getting old
Both were on the porch rocking
How they met they retold

As I was takin me evenin walk
I heard someone a yellin something
You were being chased by a hawk
He swooped at you on dreaded wing

At the same time I ran into you
There you were a leprechaun at my feet
The hawk was scared, away he flew
That was sure some way to meet

I'm glad I was there for your sake
But friends we are that's true
Well, Darby you have one wish to make
Corklin, I wish to live with you

Brolons

My name is Keyon
An elfin warrior am I
Riding a flying dragon, Fawn
Battling enemies in the sky

Venus is where I live
Battling with an alien race
Neither kingdom wanting to forgive
Brolons never showing their face

They hide behind mask and ship
Wanting to rule every world
With cruel power, gun and whip
Waiting to strike like a snake curled

With magic and power we fight back
We must destroy this enemy at any cost
Pushing them into a space hole so black
There the Brolons ships are lost

Sealing the hole with a final spell
The war is finally won at last
We hear the ringing of the victory bell
The time of danger is now past

Cabin in the Woods

My family went to cut fire wood
Taking a road we had never been on
Our last load to get if we could
Dad stopped so we could see a fawn

Dad shut the pickup off, it wouldn't start
He raised the hood, it still wouldn't run
Looking around we saw an odd looking cart
Walking to a cabin, the knocker was a sun

It looked pretty deserted but we knocked anyway
Opening the door, a man dressed in red
The jolly old man would help without delay
Please, don't worry, I'll send my mechanic, Fred

We were surprised and amazed all afternoon
Dad prescribed some medicine for a sick deer
We were going home all too soon
Going back to the cabin, it's not there!

House Hunting

Oh my! What is a cricket to do?
Mrs. Roach, has moved into my house
Grasshopper said, maybe you should sue
I even know a good lawyer, Mr. Mouse

I can't do that! She has fifty kids
Well, then what are you going to do?
Shh! Keep your head, can't flip our lids
I'll just have to live with you

Sorry, but I have no home yet
Oh no! We had better get to looking
Soon they saw a sign, Rooms to Let
Widow Spider, was out front doing her cooking

They hurried off in search of another place
Cricket said, I'll never go on vacation again!
There's Beetle! It's good to see your face
Thank you! Friend for taking us in

Magic Time

I went to explore for awhile
My mind was not on my studies today
Wizard Quebert, was teaching me of the Nile
He finally said, Merlin go out and play

It was a warm fall day
I went inside a giant cave
I went down quite a way
Torch in hand, I tried to be brave

I found what looked like a dragon egg
I wondered where his mother was
An owl was there, it had a hurt leg
Owl spoke, Dragon mother is gone, just cause

I found out both owl and dragon could talk
They were with me tell the end of time
Baby dragon hatched, was white, his name is Valk
Archimedes is the owl, both friends are prime

Majestic Mountains

The mystery of the mountains
So majestic and high
With your eternal fountains
Trees whisper your sigh

Your face sky ward
Looking into Heaven as if
Talking to the Lord
Standing still and stiff

Ageless with time are you
Standing since time began
Where animals live too
Hardly seen by man

Old man of the mountain waits
One day woken by a quake
Unknown are those dates
Sleeping tell he can wake

Michael's Brigade

Dark evil had come this way
From beyond the spirit world
But only at night they stray
At men they have been hurled

Shadows waiting to strike
To drag men down to a dark realm
Something horrid, ugly, to our dislike
Evil power to man's fate, to overwhelm

Shimmers of light unseen by eye
Coming from the corners of Heaven itself
Fighting the evil with thunderous cry
Looking like angels or winged elf

To protect man from an awful fate
Unknown to humans they exist
Only a chosen few who see and wait
Clashing battle with powerful fist

A war gone on through the ages
Good striking evil to send them away
Written in a great book of golden pages
Good keeping evil in this battle at bay

Pirate Ships

I'm a pirate captain, Zorrina is my name
I fly with The Pirate Nebulon Force
To our world an alien race came
Killing my people with little remorse

We lost the last great fight
But we won't lose this one
Our enemies has given us some insight
For we have stolen their great gun

The enemy's ships we did blast
More of their ships joined them
So we had to retreat and fast
The battle at that point looked grim

We gathered what men we could find
Weapons were also in short supply
Some of our pirates would hit from behind
Positioning, the great gun for one last try

Turning to fight, we blasted them all
Jumping on board enemy sh ips we did steal
The great gun boomed, seeing our enemies fall
Victory at last!I Zorrina at the wheel

Shadow Riders

On a dark and moonless night, Shadow Riders ride
Thundering down the road, unseen by mortal eye
Riding on the wind to turn the tide
Ever fighting against evil, they fly

Armed with shield and sword at the ready
Riding on horses breathing fire and gnashing steel
On to the battle they ride on steady
They ride on with their master's seal

Riding on down the hill to the battle
Horns blow, clashing of steel and screaming of horses
Shadow Riders fight the evil back as swords rattle
Fighting on, driving evil back with great forces

They keep battling on through the night
Destiny rides on the wind, showing the way
Clashing of swords, evil screams and takes to flight
Shadow riders, ride until there needed another day

Sleeping Giants

When the earth was new
Giants of stone walked about
Here they lived, played and grew
They were all strong and stout

Their world was full of heat
They drank from the lava stream
Volcanoes fire was good to eat
Burning ash was like their ice cream

Smoke they would breathe it
Earth was such a wonderful place
Coals would keep their homes well lit
Vapor clouds played in their face

The stone giants' time was over too soon
As the earth changed into cool fountains
Sleeping ever sleeping under a new full moon
Sleeping stone giants become our hills and mountains

Summoned

Running through the darken wood
I did not know from who
In front of me a huge mansion stood
Pulling me inside out of its view

A woman appeared in front of me
Mystic! I'm so glad you are here
Golna, my brother has turned evil, you see
He is destroying everyone, I fear

Golna has taken my powers
So I am trapped in this house
Dorsa, we need spells from the Black Towers
And we must be quiet as a mouse

Dorsa, watched as I chanted spells
I sent bolts of magic everywhere
Golna was outside with his evil Ells
Golna, was being trapped in a magical snare

Battling for three days, it was finally over
Golna was trapped and Dorsa was free
Mystic! Thank you! I can go back to Tover
Goodbye! Disappearing, to my quest in realm, Voralee

Swordsman

Running through the woods, sword in hand
Too many of them to fight this day
The King needed to know what they had planned
I had to escape, I had to get away

My heart was racing, I climbed a tree
Hoping my escape plan would work
They passed by, down I came to flee
Silently, never knowing where the enemy may lurk

Staying in the shadows, I untied my horse
I had a very long way to ride
I kept to cover and set my course
Suddenly! Two men were riding by my side

I'm glad I found you, to the King!
I explained to my friends what I'd done
We saved the King by telling him everything
One for all and all for one!

The Little Farm

A little farm house stood
Under the giant oak tree
Farther on was a stand of wood
Animals lived there so very free

In a vegetable garden was
A very lonely looking scarecrow
Scaring crows that's what he does
At night home he will go

Stopping by the pumpkin patch
Saying hello to the mouse family there
Walking on home, he lifted the latch
On the table a pie from Mrs. Bear

Supper is almost ready, dear
Scarecrow kissed his loving wife
Mrs. Mouse sent back your sewing gear
We have such a wonderful life

Trumpets Sound

As the trumpets sound
Dragons fill the air
To the castle they bound
The King had called them there

The kingdom was in danger
The magic crystal was gone
Stolen by a mysterious stranger
The dragons would go at dawn

King's men searched on the ground
Dragons searched in the air
Hoping the crystal would be found
The trail led to the witch's lair

Fighting the witch with the wizard's staff
She was sent to another place
Dragons got the crystal, with a laugh
Once again safe in its case

War Barnyard Style

Sir! There's war on
What! A war you say
Yes, I heard it from farmer, John
Then spread the word today

Off he waddled to tell everyone
The Canadian Geese flew off in fright
German Otters said, War is no fun
French Poodles hid from sight

The Russian Polecats are not our friends
But, The English Duck Brigade is ready
Bombs have been made by the hens
The horses and cows are standing steady

Iraqi Camels surrendered Sir and want to fight
Make sure it's not a trap
The Camels fought with them, with great might
Later the bears rolled out their map

Sir! Joining us are some Seals
And flying in are the Eagles
Red Cross Goats are passing out meals
We have parachute jumpers, American Beagles

The pigs have made camouflage huts
The raccoons have weapons and tanks
Let's go troops and really kick some butts
As General Fox marched through his ranks

Hidden World

Deep in the darkest of wood
A hidden city of ancient time
For many years it has stood
Getting to the city is a steep climb

As if time stood still
People still live the same way
They work here with a will
Here they seem to want to stay

Life is hard but simple
Working and living together
Still going into their temple
Their crops still depend on the weather

One leader running their world
Forgotten from everyone else's sight
As if they had been hurled
In time's hidden light

Heather

Flying through the air, I was in a hurry
I should of left earlier, that's no doubt
There's the mouse family, in their surrey
Mrs. Owl, was coming with her son, Bout

I had taken Mrs. Wren some soup
Her little girl was feeling under the weather
Dr. Mole's medicine, was some kind of goop
I hope your well soon, Good luck, Heather

I hurried on, boy! Was I in trouble
Finally, reaching Fairyland, I found my Mother
Heather! Oh dear! Get ready on the double
Dressed, I took the arm of my brother

Standing in front of my Father the king
He gave me my duty and my crown
Princess Heather! You will learn medicine on the wing
Let! The ball begin! Can't keep a princess down

Forgotten Garden

One beautiful red rose
Surrounded by weeds and thorn
She sits in her regal pose
Forgotten but not forlorn

She looks at a castle wall
Where knights once stood
And people would call
Selling wares if they could

She still dreams of that time
It was so long ago
No more music or rhyme
She hears only the wind blow

A forgotten garden in a magical land
One beautiful red rose waits
She hopes for someone with little demand
Oh! Do I hear someone at the gates?

Durkin's Quest

The yellow eyes peered in the night
Watching and waiting for something
He kept himself out of sight
On one claw he wore a gold ring

Twisting the ring, he suddenly disappeared
The space knight reappeared in his own time
He was nigh there Horace, as we feared
I waited but only found his trail slime

Get some rest Durkin, you'll need it
I'll investigate where Zorleck went
Waking later, I knew I couldn't quit
On Zorleck's trail, following the slimy yellowish tint

Finding Zorleck and his men, I silently crept
I found no guards at Zorleck's base
Luring Zorleck and his men, a trap they stepped
Putting the Planet Destroyer, back in its place

Durkin? How did you ever catch him?
I told Zorleck, I had a Megatron Laser
Zorleck tried to steal it in the dim
He sprung my trap and I grabbed his phaser

Cloud Racers

Little angels up in Heaven
Were wondering what to do
A new game was played with seven
We want to play, said the other two

Your too little and will get hurt
Argue as they might they couldn't play
They heard the horn blow to be alert
The others didn't hear, two left without delay

Cloud Racers reporting sir, what's the matter?
We have some children lost in the woods
They got in a cloud shaped like a platter
Here's your map, pull up your hoods

Two Cloud Racers, saved the children that day
The children told of two with gold rings
Seven were scolded and sent to pray
You two little angels have earned your wings

Dragon Tears

On a planet far, far away
Fairytale creatures there is no lack
To defend the castle night and day
Knights fly on dragons' back

Knights gather as trumpets call
They do as their king' commands
Dragons are readied in the stall
Weapons are gathered to defend their lands

Enemies are at the gate
Knights on dragons take to the sky
Every creature fights not knowing their fate
Each one gives their battle cry

Many days the battle raged on
Save our precious Dragon Tears, at any cost
The enemy soon fled as the battle was won
Without our Dragon Tears, we would be lost

Fishin' Hole

Sitting by a brook
It's a lazy summer day
So I dropped my hook
Here all day I'd stay

I had no real bait
No fish would I catch
But I would still wait
Lightening my pipe, I struck a match

A rainbow trout jumped
I caught a few flies
A beaver tail thumped
Laughing, at little ducks swimming tries

It was quite a frog's life
I whistled a little tune
Soon, I'd go home to my wife
I waved to Mrs. Coon

Where Evil Lurks

A monster of evil is locked away
Locking the monster up was right and good
Sitting in his prison, plotting evil each day
Laughing at the fools, pulling up his hood

I had seen what this monster could do
I desperately tried to convince all of them
They said, he's locked away, he can't hurt you
No one believed my story things looked grim

Spellbound people like statues of misunderstanding
Cheering the monster as they set him free
Smiling, his eyes were bitter, walked off the landing
The monster soon walked right past me

It wasn't very long and the monster struck
He went wild for the craving of blood
This time would be different, with any luck
Several days, finding the cave, littered with crud

I checked my gear, taking out my bow
Placing a silver arrow in its place
The vampire turned, I let my arrow go
Staring bitterly, I saw the death on his face

Whispering Wind

There is a wind that I know
It whispers of a coming storm
It's calling me to hurry and go
I stay by my fire where it's warm

The wind roars and complains outside
Smiling, I stir my cooking pot
In the morning light then I will ride
For in the storm I'll not be caught

A wanderer of lost worlds, am I
But this world is my home
The wind moaned as if to cry
My house is a cozy dome

Lightning flashes as I crawl in bed
The wind gives one more haunting try
But I am sleeping soundly, instead
Morning the storm is gone, away I fly

What Lies Beneath

Now dark and lonely street
I used to walk without delay
Once a busy city beat
All gone in one day

We are called an alien race
Alive or dead we knew not
We strive for perfection in any case
We were not a bad lot

Stories now told from place to place
Our world we did destroy
We are out of time and space
Knowledge, we used as a toy

Atlantis is the city's name
Now in the ocean deep
Fallen city with all its fame
Here is where I sleep

Wild Storm

Lightning flashes in the night sky
Dark clouds cover a full moon
Storm raged on as it did fly
North wind blew like a monsoon

Thunder boomed to sound the way
Rain came down in angry sheets
Trees were tossed in frantic sway
Rivers staying in their banks, took great feats

Boulders were being thrown like bombs to the ground
Hail hit with great force on houses below
People and animals were all safe and sound
Their signal lights made a faint glow

The storm raged on through the night
Like a wild animal trying to stand
The storm was over with the morning light
Soon the sun would dry the land

Wild Thing

The call of the wild
The meaning, what could it be?
Where cell phones aren't dialed
Howling werewolves, we may see

Vampires coming out at night
Or witches flying their brooms
Ghosts seen of golden light
Mummies dancing in their tombs

Don't forget a bigfoot or two
Chasing Frankenstein down a hill
Where dark and loathsome creatures flew
The sounds in the night aren't still

Skeletons walking down the lane
You may see a troll behind a tree
Monsters laughing like they're insane
It just sounds like home to me

Wisteria

The crystal palace was a mad house
Princess Wisteria, was to be crowned queen
Everyone was excited for the young mouse
Wisteria was the first to rule at seventeen

Her father, the King, had become quite ill
He was still going to advise her
Wisteria dressed with help from Lil
Looking in the mirror, she smoothed her fur

The King said, Wisteria would have to marry
Princess Wisteria, you have two months to wed
You must choose or marry, Duke Zarry
Then I will place the crown on your head

She loved Judd, one not of royal blood
Announcing, the bachelors! They came from all around
Princess! Duke Zarry, he was her beloved Judd!
Wisteria and Judd were married and both were crowned

Guardians at the Gate

Guardians at the gate
Huge statues in stone
Protecting the unknown fate
Cold staring alone

Their swords at hand
Like soldiers from view
Guarding this misty land
Trying to fool you

They want a password
Wrong answer will kill
Right you're free as a bird
Matching every skill

Watching for all time
Coming to life with a roar
Gate opens with a rhyme
Guardians of Heaven's door

Zarlonia

A story is told
Of a planet so rare
In times precious fold
Magic was everywhere

Everyone lives in the air
A castle and kingdom of glass
Rivers and animals are there
The planet Zarlonia has magical gas

Four powerful wizards protect it
WindWaker, controls the wind
DragonsBreath, knows where enemies will hit
StormCaller, has storms to bend

EaglesScream, keeps the magic hidden
Wizards traveling through time and space
Evil they are never ridden
But people are happy in this place